Love is in the morning when
you wake and smile at me.

Love is when we talk together,
happy as can be.

Sometimes love is quiet
and it needs no words at all.

Love is there
to catch you
when you are
about to fall.

Love is when we huddle close
and shelter from a shower.

Love is when
we take the
time to stop and
smell a flower.

I love you when you get it right, and when you get it wrong.

The world is
much more lovely
since the day you
came along.

I love you so

and when I try to count

the reasons why . . . .

. . . I find there are more reasons . . .

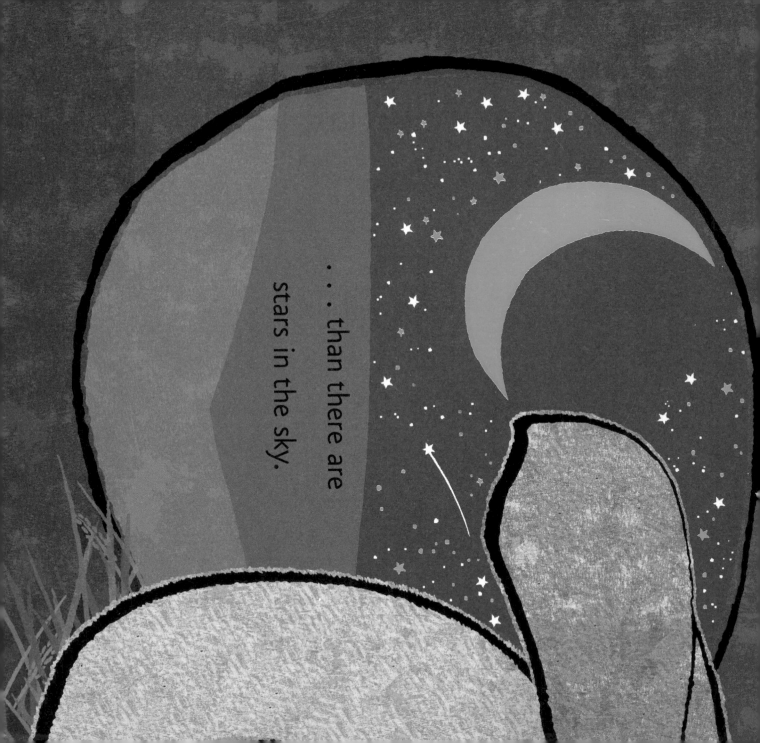

. . . than there are stars in the sky.